Batpants the orang-u

Bol

Cou

D0351976

Join Tilly and her brothers, Finn and Zak,

DEATH

for a hairy new adventure –
hoo hoo hooey hoo!

Jeremy Strong once worked in a bakery, putting the jam into three thousand doughnuts every night. Now he puts the jam in stories instead, which he finds much more exciting. At the age of three, he fell out of a first-floor bedroom window and landed on his head. His mother says that this damaged him for the rest of his life and refuses to take any responsibility. He loves writing stories because he says it is 'the only time you alone have complete control and can make anything happen'. His ambition is to make you laugh (or at least snuffle). Jeremy Strong lives near Bath with his wife, Gillie, four cats and a flying cow.

Are you feeling silly enough to read more?

BATPANTS!

THE BEAK SPEAKS

BEWARE! KILLER TOMATOES

CARTOON KID

CARTOON KID – SUPERCHARGED!

CHICKEN SCHOOL

CHRISTMAS CHAOS FOR THE HUNDRED-MILE-AN-HOUR DOG

DINOSAUR POX

DOCTOR BONKERS!
(A Cosmic Pyjamas Adventure)

GIANT JIM AND THE HURRICANE

THE HUNDRED-MILE-AN-HOUR DOG

KRANKENSTEIN'S CRAZY HOUSE OF HORROR
(A Cosmic Pyjamas Adventure)

KRAZY COW SAVES THE WORLD – WELL, ALMOST

LOST! THE HUNDRED-MILE-AN-HOUR DOG

MY BROTHER'S FAMOUS BOTTOM

MY BROTHER'S HOT CROSS BOTTOM

THERE'S A PHARAOH IN OUR BATH!

JEREMY STRONG'S LAUGH-YOUR-SOCKS-OFF JOKE BOOK
JEREMY STRONG'S LAUGH-YOUR-SOCKS-OFF EVEN MORE JOKE BOOK

LAUGH YOUR SOCKS OFF WITH

Jeremy STRONG

Batpants

and the Vanishing Elephant

Illustrated by Rowan Clifford

PUFFIN

PUFFIN BOOKS

Published by the Penguin Group

Penguin Books Ltd, 80 Strand, London WC2R 0RL, England

Penguin Group (USA) Inc., 375 Hudson Street, New York, New York 10014, USA

Penguin Group (Canada), 90 Eglinton Avenue East, Suite 700, Toronto, Ontario, Canada M4P 2Y3

(a division of Pearson Penguin Canada Inc.)

Penguin Ireland, 25 St Stephen's Green, Dublin 2, Ireland (a division of Penguin Books Ltd)

Penguin Group (Australia), 250 Camberwell Road, Camberwell, Victoria 3124, Australia

(a division of Pearson Australia Group Pty Ltd)

Penguin Books India Pvt Ltd, 11 Community Centre, Panchsheel Park, New Delhi – 110 017, India

Penguin Group (NZ), 67 Apollo Drive, Rosedale, Auckland 0632, New Zealand

(a division of Pearson New Zealand Ltd)

Penguin Books (South Africa) (Pty) Ltd, 24 Sturdee Avenue, Rosebank, Johannesburg 2196, South Africa

Penguin Books Ltd, Registered Offices: 80 Strand, London WC2R 0RL, England

puffinbooks.com

First published 2011

001 – 10 9 8 7 6 5 4 3 2 1

Text copyright © Jeremy Strong, 2011

Illustrations copyright © Rowan Clifford, 2011

All rights reserved

The moral right of the author and illustrator has been asserted

Set in Baskerville

Made and printed in Great Britain by Clays Ltd, St Ives plc

British Library Cataloguing in Publication Data

A CIP catalogue record for this book is available from the British Library

ISBN: 978-0-141-32797-6

www.greenpenguin.co.uk

MIX
Paper from
responsible sources
FSC® C018179
www.fsc.org

Penguin Books is committed to a sustainable
future for our business, our readers and our
planet. This book is made from paper certified
by the Forest Stewardship Council.

This is for all those working to save
threatened animals around the world,
and in particular for all orang-utans,
especially any that can read.

Contents

1. An Unexpected Delivery of Fudge   1

2. Zak Goes Down on His Knees   17

3   Who is Manky Pup?   28

4. Fudge Cakes   46

5. Manley's Busy Day   60

6. Fantasti-bubbly-crumbo!   76

7. Batpants on the Trail   91

8. Disaster Strikes   107

9. All About Thursday   120

10. Surprised? You're Telling Me!   139

1 An Unexpected Delivery of Fudge

The first thing I saw was the post van. Well, it wasn't actually a van, it was a lorry. A large post office lorry with double wheels at the back and everything. Finn was busy showing me his best caterpillar at the time. He has five caterpillars at the moment, plus three spiders, several woodlice and an earwig called Thursday, because it was a Thursday when Finn found it.

I asked if it was morning or afternoon when he discovered it and Finn said afternoon, so I said maybe he should call it *Thursday Afternoon*. Finn looked at me as if I was an idiot, which was a bit much coming from someone who definitely *is* an idiot and certainly WEIRD.

How many people do you know who go around with their pockets stuffed full of beetles and wriggly things? Exactly. Weird.

Finn is my little brother. He's seven, which means he's a child, as opposed to me. I'm ten, which is almost teenage and therefore grown-up. Finn gets very excited by small squiggly things and ginormous noisy things, so you can imagine how hyper he got when he saw the post office lorry. Finn said it was the biggest lorry he had ever seen, ever, EVER.

We watched from the window as a big, hairy guy with tattoos all over his arms got out and came to our door.

'Delivery. Sign here,' he said and Dad scribbled on Hairy Guy's electronic pad.

'Why are lorry drivers fat?' Finn asked. I tried telling him they weren't.

'Yes, they are,' he insisted. 'All the ones I've seen are fat.'

'OK, so now you're a fat-lorry-driver spotter

are you? Anyhow, look, there's another man
from the lorry. He's not fat.'

'He's not the driver,' Finn said. HE IS *SUCH*
A KNOW-ALL! I gave up. What's the point in
arguing if you can't win?

The second man opened up the back of the
lorry. He pressed some buttons and a long ramp
slid out of the back and down to the road.

'That's a very big lorry for one small letter,'
I muttered. Finn looked up at me with his big,
serious eyes and shook his head.

'It can't be a letter. It's got to be something
MEGA-MASSIVE. I bet it's an elephant!'

'Oh yeah, people are always posting elephants
to each other, aren't they? They probably say
things like "I'm just going down the road to pop
an elephant in the post."'

Finn looked at me coldly. 'You're stupid,' he
grumbled.

'And you're very small and your brain is even
smaller,' I shot back. 'In fact I can't see it, not
even with the world's most powerful microscope.'

At that moment I felt something very warm
and hairy on my arm. It was an orang-utan
hand. Yes, I know it's unusual to have an orang-
utan in the house but, there you go, that's what
our house is like – orang-utans everywhere. Well,
to be honest, we only have one, but Batpants *gets*
everywhere so it often seems as if we have loads.

Batpants is one of our pets. We have lots of animals around because our dad is an amazingly brilliant animal trainer. His name is Aslan and he trains animals for films and TV. He's the best animal trainer IN THE WORLD, and I'm not exaggerating. Anyhow, Batpants was orphaned when she was very young and Dad looked after her and now she lives in our house.

Actually, she mostly lives in the tree house that Dad built for us out in the garden. It's brilliant! We've each got our own room, even Batpants, and that's where Finn and Zak and I live too.

You don't know about Zak yet do you? I shall try not to mention him too much because he's a pain. This is all you need to know about Zak.

1. He's just turned fourteen and is therefore a teenager and dangerous.

2. He's moody. (He's a teenager.)

3. He's argumentative. (He's a teenager.)

4. He's very tidy. (He's a – hang on, teenagers aren't meant to be tidy!)

5. He plays guitar very loudly in a band called The Non-Organic Vegetables.

6. His hair is black and purple. (It's been dyed. Plus, he's got a stud on his left eyebrow.)

7. He's ALWAYS falling in love. If you put a celery stick in front of him he'd probably fall in love with it. (It wouldn't surprise me if he ran away and married it. Then they could be Mr and Mrs Celery.)

8. He's going to be famous, he says. (Yeah – for marrying a vegetable!)

Anyhow, back to the post office lorry. Batpants was slowly climbing up on to my shoulders, which is quite nice but she does weigh an awful lot. Plus, she tries to hold on to you by wrapping her hairy hands round your eyes, or across your mouth, or up your nose — she doesn't care, as long as you can't see or breathe.

Both the postmen were now in the back of the lorry and so was Dad. We heard a lot of thumping and banging and the lorry shuddered as if it was about to sneeze. Then Dad came and stood in the road to make sure there were no cars about.

Finally, the postmen reappeared, pulling a long rope. They kept shouting at whatever it was inside the lorry.

'Come on!'

'You can't stay in there forever!'

'Here kitty-kitty!'

Kitty-kitty? Was there a cat in there? That wouldn't make everything rattle about, surely?

Then the ramp on the road banged and buckled and shuddered beneath the weight, and slowly, bit by bit, out came –

'It IS an elephant!' yelled Finn, jumping up and down. 'I said it was an elephant, didn't I? I said it and you told me my brain was too small, but I was right and you were wrong and that means you're a poo-head.'

'Thank you,' I murmured. Well, how was I supposed to guess it was an elephant? How many times do you get elephant deliveries at *your* house?

It's not what you expect, is it?

So, this elephant comes trundling down the ramp and on to the road, slowly swinging its trunk and gently flapping its ears, and that was when I saw the address and the stamps. There they were, on the side of the elephant – Dad's name and address plus three hundred and seventy-eight stamps (we counted them). That's an awful lot of stamps.

I felt a sudden, terrible pain on my head. It was Batpants. She was thumping the top of my skull with her fists, like a drum, and shouting 'Hoo hoo hooey hoo!' very loudly in my left ear.

I pulled her off my back. She immediately began running round in circles, which was very awkward for me because she grabbed my hand. Basically, I was spun round four times and just when I thought my arm would probably get twisted right off, I fell over.

'Batpants! Get off me, you hairy ginger monster!'

'Hoo hah! Hoo hah! Chk-chk-chk-chk-chk!'

Batpants does this mad chattering thing when she's excited and she was certainly excited by the elephant. Maybe the elephant reminded of her of her own country. They've got elephants in Borneo, which is where Batpants came from. She was going so bonkers you'd think she'd just found a long lost auntie or something. Maybe it *was* her long lost auntie!

The postmen packed up the back of the lorry and off they went (with the fat one driving), while Dad slowly walked the elephant into our back garden, or maybe it was the other way round, with the elephant walking Dad. It was difficult to tell.

The elephant stood there, surrounded by the whole family because Mum and Zak had appeared now. We all stood there looking at the elephant and admiring the three hundred and seventy-eight stamps and the elephant stood there looking at us with her small, crinkly, twinkly eyes. She seemed cool, calm and collected. Dad made the introductions.

'This is Fudge,' he announced. 'The elephant,' he added, unnecessarily, in case we hadn't noticed.

'I'd never have guessed, Dad,' said Zak. 'I thought she was a tortoise.'

Finn went into hysterics, pointing at Fudge and spluttering 'It's a tortoise! A big, BIG tortoise with a trunk! No, no, it's a tortephant!'

Dad smiled patiently. 'Fudge is going to be with us for about a month while I train her for a film. She's a lovely beast, and pretty clever too.'

Batpants was pulling me forward. She was fascinated and wanted to get closer. The orang-utan slowly reached out with a long arm, poked the elephant gently with one finger and leapt back in case the beast sat on her.

Fudge didn't even blink. She just swung her trunk a little more, curled it round Batpants and gently lifted the orang-utan on to her back. Batpants was in heaven! She sat there with an enormous grin on her face, showing all her very white teeth. She obviously thought she'd just been made Queen of the Universe.

'Fudge is a gentle giant,' Dad chuckled. 'She's going to be easy to train.'

'What film will she be in?' I asked. 'Will it be one of Mum's *Colorado Kate* movies?'

Dad shook his head. 'No. Your mother won't be in this one.'

I should explain about Mum. She's a stuntwoman! Most of her work is for a TV series called *Colorado Kate*. Kate is always falling off a building or fighting wolves or tumbling over the edge of waterfalls – all that crazy, dangerous stuff. The actress who plays Kate is way too important to do her own stunts so Mum does them for her.

We were still standing there staring at Fudge and Batpants when there was a shout from the side of the house.

'Hello! Anyone there?'

'We're in the garden!' Dad shouted. 'Make your way round!'

We all turned and gazed expectantly at the corner of the house.

2   Zak Goes Down on His Knees

A moment later
a young girl
appeared. I say
'young', but I
guess she was
maybe fifteen
or sixteen,
dressed in a
loose shirt, with
her jeans tucked
into wellies.
She was quite
pretty too and
I immediately
shot a glance at
Zak. Oh, yes.

Groan, groan. He was already overcome. He was practically on his knees proposing marriage. Well, no, of course he wasn't, but you Know What I Mean. Boys. What can you do?

The girl flashed a smile at all of us that was so dazzling I almost went blind. Good grief – what did she have in her mouth – searchlights?

'Hi, I'm India. I see you've already met my elephant, Fudge.' India reached up and patted the elephant's flank. 'Hello, sweetie – good to see you again. Who's a booful gorgeous girl, did you have a safe journey? And oh, who's this beauty then?' India asked, reaching up to Batpants. 'Hey, aren't you a cutie-pie!' India spoke in a breathy, hushed voice, like a comfy pillow.

Finn nudged me hard. 'India is VERY STRANGE, isn't she?' he whispered, stroking his pet earwig. 'I think she's probably a bit, you know, bonkers.'

I was almost ready to agree with him, but Zak obviously didn't care how bonkers India was. He had been knocked out by her megazonic, billion dollar, diamond smile.

Meanwhile, Dad was introducing everyone. 'I'm Aslan,' Dad said. 'I've heard a lot about you, all of it good. This is my wife, Emma, and this bunch of lunatics is all our own work – Zak, Tilly and Finn.'

We all stood there grinning at each other in a rather embarrassed kind of way until Dad hastily went on.

'India is Fudge's keeper,' he explained. 'She's looked after Fudge for the last three years. India will be staying with us until I finish Fudge's training.'

'She'll be staying with us?' repeated Zak, as if he'd just won the lottery. 'Cool.' He flicked back his long hair and smiled at India. 'You must be very clever.'

Huh. Nice try, Zak! But India only had eyes for Fudge. She was looking at all the stamps on the elephant's side. 'We can't have you looking like that, popsicle. That's no way for a lady to dress.' She swung round and asked dad if he had a hose and broom. He nodded and went off to the shed.

In case you're wondering why my dad is called Aslan, it's because he's Turkish. Aslan is a common name in Turkey and it means 'lion'. That's what my Dad is like; he's got a big mane of hair for a start and, and, well, now I come to think of it that is the *only* way in which he's like a lion. I mean, he doesn't have claws or sharp teeth, and he doesn't pounce on people and eat them. In fact he's the kindest man ever, which is probably why he's so good at training animals.

Dad came back and handed over the hose and broom, fixing the other end of the hose to the outside tap.

India reached up to Batpants. 'Come on, sweety-pops. You'd better get down from there, honey-babe, or you're going to get a bit wet.'

'Hooey hoo, ha, chk-chk-chk-chk!' chattered Batpants, windmilling her arms and trying to drive India away. The orang-utan wasn't having any of it. Her Majesty was going to stay put on her elephantine throne.

'I don't think honey-babe wants to play,' I murmured to Finn and he giggled.

'OK,' sighed India. 'But don't blame me if you get soaked. OK, Aslan, turn it on.'

The hose gave a few gurgles and shakes, a dribble of water flopped out lazily and then –

SWOOOOOOOOSSSHHHH!!

Water splurged from the hose as if it was being chased by a million thirsty buffaloes. It thundered against Fudge's flanks, drenching her from top to toe. The elephant lifted her trunk and blew a very happy fanfare – BLAARRR – DE – BLAAARRRRR!

Batpants wasn't nearly so happy. She ran, shrieking, backwards and forwards along the elephant's back. She waved her arms furiously in the air, bared her teeth and screamed at everyone. I think she was trying to say 'Help! I'm soaking wet. Get me down from here!' What actually came out her mouth was –

'YEEEEEEEEEEEEEEEEE!!!'

Meanwhile she carried on getting soaked, while India aimed the water at all the stamps. One by one they were blasted off until all were gone, and that just left the address. India scrubbed away with the broom until that vanished too. Finally, she went all round the big beast giving her a good hose down. Fudge loved every minute of it. Batpants didn't, and when Dad eventually turned off the hose Batpants collapsed in a soggy heap on top of Fudge's head. She looked like an enormous, orange, overused mop. And very wet.

India laughed. 'Don't say I didn't warn you, Batpants. Now, are you going to come down?'

Batpants pushed out her lower lip, curled it down and pulled the sulkiest face ever, so India turned to the elephant for help. 'Fudge, sweetheart, could you get Batpants down for us? She really needs to dry off.'

Fudge flapped her ears a couple of times, reached up with her trunk, collected the giant, limp, orange mop and gently put her on the

ground. Batpants lay there on her back in a
spreading pool of water, her limbs flopped out in
starfish fashion. She looked like a cross-channel
swimmer who'd just been rescued from drowning.

I have to say I was pretty impressed at the way India and Fudge seemed to understand each other. She may be completely dippy-daft but she certainly knew how to deal with elephants.

Mum nipped into the house and reappeared with a couple of old towels. India set to, rubbing Batpants all over while she lay on the ground and moaned as if she was dying. The more India rubbed the more Batpants groaned.

'*Urrrrrrrrgh! Urrrrrrrgh! URRRRRRRGGHHHH!*'

That orang-utan is such an actress! She's even better than star-of-the-silver-screen, Victoria Sponge – though not quite as attractive, unless of course you're an orang-utan too.

India threw the other towel across to Zak. For a few seconds he stared down at it and then he launched into action. He strode forward, got down on his knees beside India – IN THE MUD – and began towelling Batpants too.

Mum and Dad and Finn and I all looked at

each other. We tried not to snigger, but it was impossible. There was Zak – the would-be rock-star, Zak the Mighty, Zak the Cool, Zak with the T-Shirt that had DEATH written across the front – there he was, on his knees, in the mud, rubbing an orang-utan with a towel.

'So sweet,' murmured Mum.

'Wish I had a camera,' Dad whispered back. He watched the pair at work for a moment. 'That

girl is a natural with animals. She'll go far. One
day she'll be a better animal trainer than me.'

'Not possible, Dad,' I snapped.

'She will, Tilly, she will. You wait and see.'

I grinned up at him. *'Oh, honey-babe!'* I mocked.
Dad laughed but Mum cut in.

'You make fun of India all you like, Tilly,'
she said. 'But who's
looking after the
elephant?'

3   Who is Manky Pup?

Everybody I know thinks it's really cool to have a mum who works in films. I suppose it is a bit. She's worked with loads of film stars and done some amazing things but there is a downside. Mum often has to go away for months. She might be filming in some faraway place.

Plus, her work is dangerous, and I mean DANGEROUS – that's why other people don't do it. Sometimes she gets hurt. I always know when she's been working on a really tough film because when she eventually gets home she goes and sleeps under the kitchen table. She reckons it's the safest place to be.

'At least I know I can't fall *off* anything and nothing will fall *on* me, either,' Mum says.

I guess the one good thing is that when Mum

is at home we enjoy it all the more. I mean, when your mum's around all the time you get so used to it you get bored and fed up. Then you start thinking things like: *hmmm, I wish my best friend's mum was MY mum. My best friend's mum is much nicer than my mum.*

Do you ever think things like that? So do I sometimes, but it's not because I'm bored with Mum, it's because I don't see her enough. I wish my mum was around all the time, like an ordinary mum.

I have to keep myself busy while Mum's away filming so I don't think about her too much, so it's a pretty good thing that I have got an awful lot to do. Saving The World is a pretty big task if you ask me, especially if you are doing it all by yourself.

I'm an eco-warrior and I am going to save the planet because that's a VERY IMPORTANT THING TO DO and none of the politicians and grown-ups in the world seem to care two fiddlesticks about it, so I am going to have to do it instead.

Actually, there are some grown-ups who worry about it, but I don't think any of them live in our street, apart from Mum and Dad. I have been trying to tell people in our road what they can do to help. I write letters on Dad's computer and print them off and then I pop them through people's letterboxes.

You wouldn't think giving someone free advice about saving the planet would get you into trouble would you? Well it does, like when I saw this man sitting in one of those gigantic 4x4 SUV jobs and I went up to him and said he shouldn't drive cars like that because they waste petrol and make lots of bad gases that go into the air and cause pollution. Do you know what he said back?

'Stop being so nosy. I am a policeman doing my job, making sure the streets are safe for children like you, so mind your own business before I arrest you and put you in jail for being a nuisance.'

That was nice, wasn't it? So it seemed like I would be Saving The Whole World minus One Policeman. I didn't like the look of him, anyhow. He had bristly hairs up the inside of his nose. It looked like an evil forest up there, complete with an evil witch and a house made of gingerbread and sweets and stuff.

Mum and Dad are very proud of me for wanting to Save The World. Finn thinks I'm daft and Zak thinks I'm crazy. But he's the crazy one. Zak wastes SO much electricity! He leaves lights on everywhere. I say to him, 'Switch it off!' And he says, 'Switch yourself off!' And he laughs because he thinks that's funny.

Huh. He won't be laughing when there's no electricity left because HE'S USED IT ALL UP – playing his electric guitar, mostly. I keep telling him he should get a clockwork one.

'Don't be an idiot. There's no such thing.' That's what he shouts.

'Why not? You can get wind-up radios and wind-up torches. Why can't you get a wind-up electric guitar? All bands should be eco-aware and only play on wind-up guitars, that's what I think'

'I keep telling you, dodo brain, there's no such thing,' shouts Zak.

'Yes, there is,' I shout back. 'I've just invented it.'

Then he starts slamming doors. Mum says

that's what teenagers usually do. 'It's a kind of sign language,' she says. 'It means *leave me alone*. At least he keeps his room tidy,' she added, meaningfully. You know what *'meaningfully'* means, don't you? It means she was having a go at me, because my room *isn't* tidy. I think tidy rooms are SO boring and clean and uncomfortable. I like a comfortable room, and that's how I keep my bedroom.

Anyway, Zak's in love with India now, so I suppose we're going to have to put up with that for the next month or so. Zak will be moping about all over the place.

Don't tell Zak, but I think India is quite nice – in a dippy-daft sort of way, of course. She wants to save the world too, only she started with elephants instead of light switches.

'Elephants are hunted for their tusks,' India told me at supper. We were all sitting at the big kitchen table.

'Nobody is supposed to hunt them. It's against the law. But evil poachers go after them and kill them and take their tusks because they can get lots of money for them. And in some countries they are made to work really hard and they aren't looked after properly. That's what happened to Fudge, the poor darling. She was forced to pull huge logs to a saw mill to be cut up for furniture and stuff.

'She got rescued by an animal charity and brought to Britain. I used to go down and help on their animal farm. Fudge and I got on really well and formed a bond. She would only trust me

to bring her food and things like that. That's how I became her keeper. I think I'm the youngest elephant keeper in the country!'

'You're so clever,' said Zak, his face full of admiration. Finn looked at me.

'Are we going to be sick?' he whispered.

'Yes,' I nodded. 'One, two, three –'

SPLURRRRGH!

Then we both sniggered. Zak turned red and scowled at us both. 'What was that about?' he demanded.

'Finn wanted to know if I'd like some more potato salad,' I answered cheerfully.

'We're not eating potato salad,' snapped Zak.

'That's OK,' I shrugged. 'I didn't want any, anyhow.'

Finn burst out giggling. I thought he was laughing at what I'd said, which was, I thought, pretty funny, but Finn pointed at Batpants, who was helping herself to the little cherry tomatoes from a bowl on the table.

'Tomato alert!' muttered Finn.

Batpants' mouth was bulging more and more as she loaded her mouth with ammunition.

Tomatoes are just about her favourite food, but
she doesn't eat them. Finn and I waited and
watched, and then it came. Suddenly Batpants
pursed her lips and –

RATTA-TATTA-SPLATTA!

Tomatoes sprayed from her mouth like
machine gun bullets and *BLAPP*! One
got Zak right on his head.
BLAPP! Another got
India on her
shoulder.

'Everyone duck!' yelled Dad, but it was too late. The damage had been done. Batpants was delighted. 'Hoo hoo haahhhh!' she chanted, standing on her chair.

'Sit down at once!' demanded Mum angrily. 'Who let Batpants get hold of those tomatoes? You know what she's like with them.'

I pulled Batpants back on to her chair and moved the bowl out of the way. India was laughing.

'She is such a character! Fudge is a bit like that too. She's a poppet, but she can do some wild things and I think she knows she's being funny. She likes a joke. I must say I was wondering why your kitchen walls are a bit, well, kind of, um –'

'Messy?' suggested Mum. 'In a tomato-pippy kind of way? Now you know why. Just make sure the tomatoes are kept well away from that ape. I don't know who allowed it to happen today, especially when we have a guest.' Mum peered round the table trying to search out the culprit. I knew I was innocent, but Finn was certainly looking guilty.

'I think my elbow may have caught the bowl a bit and, maybe, sort of, pushed it, in her direction, possibly. But it wasn't deliberate,' he added quickly. 'It was an accident.'

'I'm gonna have to wash my hair now,' Zak grumbled. 'It takes ages to dry,' he added, his voice like stone.

We all looked at him, even India, who was trying to keep a straight face.

'Poor Zak,' Mum tried to say without cracking up, and India bit her lip even more. I just stared at the tablecloth. I thought, *if I catch anyone's eye now I shall just burst into a gazillion giggles*.

'OK, settle down everyone,' said Dad, trying to restore a bit of calm. 'Sorry about that, India. It doesn't usually happen.'

'You know what they say in films,' smiled India. 'Never work with children or animals.'

'Quite right too,' said Mum. 'I wonder which is worse. The children or the animals?'

'Animals!' we all shouted, just as Dad said 'Children!'

He went on. 'Listen up, I have some news for you. We're going to have another guest with us for a while. Fudge is here to be trained up for this new comedy movie. That means she's going to work closely with one of the stars of the film. So the actor is going to be here for a while so Fudge can get used to it.'

Finn and Zak and I stared at Dad.

'A film star is coming here, to stay?' asked Zak.

'Yes.'

'Who?' I shouted. 'Who is it? Frangelika Wotnot?'

Dad shook his head and looked round the table at our expectant faces.

'Is it Victoria Sponge?' Zak suggested. (One of his favourites, of course.)

Dad shook his head again. 'It's Manley Strutt.'

So guess who almost fainted? Mum! And me
a bit too. I mean, Manley Strutt! Even Batpants
was impressed. She sat at the table, arms draped
over her head, shaking her face so her big lips
wobbled slobbily.

'Blubble-ubble-ubble-ubble-blurrrrrgh!'

Dad was looking at Mum with a worried
expression. She kept whispering 'Manley Strutt'
over and over again as if she couldn't believe it.
She reached out a hand and put it on Dad's arm.
'Manley Strutt,' she repeated, looking right into
Dad's eyes. 'He's almost as handsome as you, but
he's not the man I love.'

Dad sighed with relief. 'I was beginning to wonder!'

Mum's fingers drummed the table for a moment. 'On the other hand, he must have a lot more money than you. Hmmmm, difficult choice.'

In the meantime, Finn was panicking. He stood there, completely puzzled and shouted. 'Will somebody please tell me: WHO IS MANKY PUP?'

Mum burst out laughing. 'Please, Finn, when this man comes to stay with us do NOT call him Manky Pup. He won't be very pleased. His name is Manley Strutt and he's played a rather hunky action hero in many films.'

'He's very handsome,' India added, putting a lot of stress on the word 'very'. Zak scowled at her, while Finn folded his arms. Neither of them were the least bit impressed, so far.

'Can he do stunts, like you?' Finn asked Mum.

'Yes. In fact he's one of the few actors who can do their own stunts.'

Finn nodded. Maybe Manley Strutt would be OK with him.

Zak sidled up to India. 'Do you want to see my guitar?' he asked. India turned to him, eyes twinkling and gave her head a little shake.

'Maybe later. Just think, Manley Strutt, staying right here, in this house, with us!'

'Yeah,' muttered Zak, his voice like a bowl of cold porridge. 'Brilliant.'

As Zak went drooping past me I tried to cheer him up. 'Never mind, Zak. India might fall head over heels in love with Manley Strutt, but there's still Fudge the elephant. Maybe you could take her out instead?'

'Shut up, dustbin-face,' he snapped back.

Dad heard us sniping at each other and sighed heavily. 'Don't you love happy families?' he asked.

Batpants went lolloping across to Dad, flung

one long arm round both his legs, reached up with her other arm and stuck two hairy fingers in his right ear.

Dad pulled her hand away. 'When I want my ears cleaning, Batpants, I will let you know. Now, there's work to be done. We need to get a room ready for Manley. India, you need to clean out Fudge. Tilly, you can help her. You like getting filthy so I'm sure you'll be more than happy to help India clear up all the elephant droppings.'

I looked at Dad, aghast. Elephant droppings? I couldn't think of anything worse. But I was in for an even bigger shock!

4   Fudge Cakes

India collects elephant droppings. Well, I
suppose everyone should have a hobby, but I was
surprised by this one. I wonder how Zak will take
it? Perhaps he'd like to help her. Ha ha! He can
hardly bear to touch a dirty dinner plate. That's
his excuse for getting out of the washing-up and
we end up quarrelling – something like this.

'Urgh! The plates are all icky.'

'But Zak – this was *your* plate. You are a
washing-up wimp.'

'And you're a GIRL,' says Zak.

'Is that the best you can do for an argument?
I'll tell you what, I have a better idea. Let's put
everything in the dishwasher.'

'That's a pretty good idea,' says Zak,
brightening up at last.

'I know. It's because I'm a GIRL,' I tell him. 'Girls have brains, you see.' And we put everything in the dishwasher and everyone's happy. What would the world do without people like me? It would probably crash into little bits, that's what.

Anyhow, as I was saying, India collects elephant droppings. That doesn't mean she picks them up and sticks them into a special book, like stamps or pressed flowers. Imagine a book full of pressed elephant dung! YURRKKKK! Although as things turned out, that wasn't far from the truth.

India told me something A-MAZING. I was watching her trudge round the garden with a bucket and spade, collecting Fudge's droppings. They're pretty big, I must say, a bit like large chocolate cakes which have just fallen from a tall building and gone SPLAT!

And here's Strange Fact Numéro Un: Elephant poo hardly smells at all because it's made almost entirely of fibre. I bet you didn't know that! (By the way, *numéro un* is French for number one. We're learning French at school, and now you are too, except you're probably at home.)

And here is Strange Fact Numéro Deux. (You've worked out what that means already, haven't you? Clever you!) Animal poo is a major source of bad gases that pollute the atmosphere. (Cows are one of the worst for this!) So if you can use the poo in a useful way it's a Very Good Thing.

And here is Strange Fact Numéro Trois. You can use elephant poo to make paper.

48

IT'S TRUE! I'M NOT TELLING PORKIES!! IT'S THE TRUTH!!!

I was watching India and she called across to me.

'Hi, sweetheart! You want to help?'

'Er, not really,' I told her, because it's not the sort of hobby that grabbed me really.

'I thought you said you're an eco-warrior?' India straightened up, flashing her strobe-light teeth at me. Aaaargh! Blinded again. 'You know, saving the world, and all that kind of thing?'

'I am,' I said, pointing to the twigs in my hair. I like dressing up in what I call 'eco-fashion'. I weave long grasses and small bits of plant into my hair and rub mud on my face – that sort of thing. It makes me feel closer to the earth. I also do it so people will know I'm into eco stuff.

India nodded. 'You look lovely, honey, but why don't you come and do something that will really help?' She waved her spade and bucket at me.

'Collecting Fudge cakes will help?' I asked.

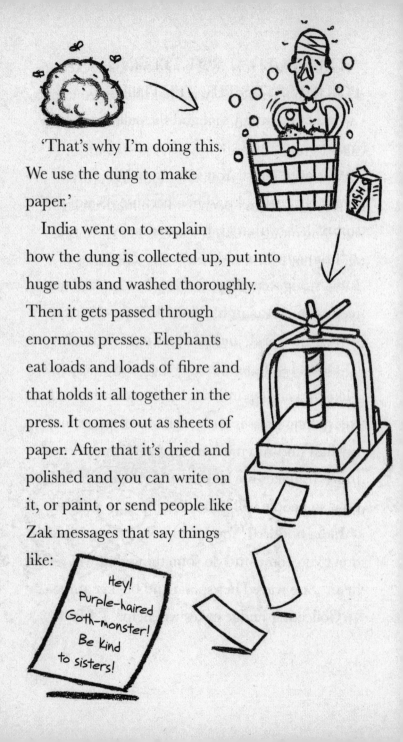

'That's why I'm doing this. We use the dung to make paper.'

India went on to explain how the dung is collected up, put into huge tubs and washed thoroughly. Then it gets passed through enormous presses. Elephants eat loads and loads of fibre and that holds it all together in the press. It comes out as sheets of paper. After that it's dried and polished and you can write on it, or paint, or send people like Zak messages that say things like:

Hey! Purple-haired Goth-monster! Be kind to sisters!

So that's how it is. You could have knocked me down with a feather when I heard that. Actually, you could have knocked me down with a Fudge cake. I grabbed another bucket and spade.

We would have got that garden tidied up in no time if it hadn't been for Batpants. She came waddling along with a bucket of her own. She followed us round trying to copy what we were doing, but most of the time she just spilt her dung back on the ground. We had to chase after her to get it. Batpants decided that was a very good game. She grabbed the dung and started scooting up the nearest tree with it. When we went anywhere near she threw it at us, which WASN'T VERY NICE.

Dad had to creep up on her from behind and grab her. He took her inside so we could carry on in peace. It took us another half hour but eventually the job was done and we ended with a high five, which would have been OK if we weren't still holding our spades, so it was more of a high SPLANGGGG!

I guess India is all right really, as long as she doesn't keep calling me 'sweetheart' and 'honey pie' and so on. She told me something else too. Zak has asked her to be in his band.

'What instrument do you play?' I asked.

'Zak says I could be really good on the tambourine.'

Huh! Tambourine, indeed. I bet Zak just wants to snog her.

I was going to warn her about Zak, but we were interrupted by the arrival of Manley Strutt. There we were, standing in the garden with our buckets of elly doo-doo, when the hunk himself arrived.

WHY WEREN'T WE WARNED?

I mean, is this the way a girl wants to be introduced to a handsome film star?

I DON'T THINK SO!

I didn't even have time to rearrange the twigs in my hair. Or put on some more mud make-up.

Anyhow, Mr Handsome Hunk of The Year comes walking into the garden, smiling from ear to there. It was a really cheesy smile too – gorgonzola probably – you know, one of the smelly ones. Manley held out a big hand to greet us.

We both held out our hands to be shaken but for some reason Manley Strutt's eyes were on our buckets instead and he backed off.

'Hey!' He grinned, and his teeth were almost as blinding as India's. 'I see you've got your hands full of – erm . . .'

'Erm?' I repeated. 'Actually it's elephant dung. We make paper with it.'

You should have seen Manley Strutt's eyes! They almost took off from his head!

'Paper?' His voice was hoarse with disbelief. 'You make paper with – *that*?'

'Yep. It's good for the planet. Recycling and all that.' I smiled brightly at him. I thought he'd be impressed with my new-found knowledge, but he just turned very pale.

'And did all that come from –' Manley left the question hovering in mid-air.

'From Fudge, our elephant? Oh yes, it's all Fudge's,' India told him. 'I guess you could say she's the manufacturer.'

'Oh boy!' wheezed Manley. 'Oh boy, oh boy! Well, there's a thing!'

And just when Manley was looking *almost* completely confused, Batpants came rushing out of the house to finish off the job.

'Hoo hoo hah hah HOOOOOOOOO!' screeched the orang-utan as she raced across the garden. She launched herself into the air and leapt on to Manley's back. (And don't forget the hands round the eyes and fingers up the nose bit.)

Manley didn't yell. He SQUEALED! He squealed like a two-year-old who's just dropped his ice cream in the road and seen it run over by six buses and a bicycle. He began to dance

a strange kind of jig, flapping his arms up and down and spinning round, trying to get the giant hairy orange rucksack off his back.

It was Mum who came to the rescue this time.

'Sorry, Mr Strutt,' she apologized. 'Batpants loves to meet new people. This is her way of saying "hello". I can tell she likes you.'

'Likes me?' repeated Manley in dismay. 'Strangling me is her way of saying she likes me?'

Mum held Manley's gaze and nodded. 'Batpants is an orang-utan, an animal. Animals have their own ways of showing their feelings and we humans just have to accept them.'

The hunk patted his hair back into place and looked about him. He sighed heavily. 'I've got to spend weeks here in this madhouse. Will I ever get out alive?'

Mum burst out laughing. 'Don't you worry. We'll take very good care of you. Come back into the house for a cup of tea.'

Manley eyed Batpants. 'Is she invited?'

'Not if you'd rather she wasn't,' said Mum. 'Although she *is* pretty good with a mug of tea. She doesn't spill much.'

'Just watch the tomatoes,' Finn piped up out of nowhere.

Manley spun round, trying to track him down, but Finn was nowhere to be seen.

'Who said that?' demanded Manley.

'I did!' cried Finn with delight, suddenly reappearing, upside down and hanging from a branch of the tree house.

'Oh, hi, kid. Good to see you. Is that some kind of camp you have there?'

'No. It's our house,' Finn explained. 'We live here.'

Manley took another deep, deep breath and turned to my mother. 'OK, so let's see if I've got this straight. You have a big ape creature that drinks tea and lives in the house, and a small son who lives in a tree in the garden? Oh boy!' He sighed again, shaking his head. 'So what's the big deal with the tomatoes?' he asked.

Mum laughed. It was what you call a 'forced' laugh. In other words she was covering up!

'Ha ha ha!' she tinkled. 'Tomatoes aren't a problem. Finn was just – just being Finn,' she finally said, shooting a warning look at my little brother.

The three of them went indoors, with Batpants holding Manley by one hand and walking with him. No, that's not quite right – Batpants wasn't *walking*, she was *dragging* Manley along, as if she was taking a prisoner to his doom.

India and I looked at each other. Life was getting very interesting.

5.   Manley's Busy Day

I don't know much about film stars. I have read about them in magazines and I know some of them can act a bit spoilt. They expect everything to be done for them. Manley wasn't like that at all, but he was surprisingly squeamish about having an orang-utan in the house.

'Oh boy,' he'd say, with a shake of his head. 'It's so – weird – you know? Sitting at the breakfast table with an orang-utan.'

'I suppose it feels like that at first,' agreed Mum. 'We're all used to it. Batpants always eats with us.'

India giggled. 'At least it isn't Fudge trying to eat with us at the table.'

'Sure,' nodded Manley, trying to look brave. 'But does she have to spread honey on her foot like that?'

'Yes, Batpants,' warned Mum. 'No feet on the table, thank you.'

'She's an ape, Manley,' Dad told him. 'I've seen humans with worse table manners.'

Manley managed a bit of a smile. 'I guess that's true. But she's putting the knife in her ear now.'

Batpants glanced at the film star, showed her teeth and tried to spread honey on his hand. 'Heeeee haaaaaa splurrrrgh!'

'Thanks, but no thanks,' Manley said quickly, while Mum carefully took the knife from the ape before she sliced off several of Manley's fingers.

Manley, still in his dressing gown, got up from the table. 'I guess I'll run myself a bath if that's OK. Somehow all the honey has made me feel a bit sticky.'

India watched him leave. 'I can't believe I've been sitting at breakfast with Manley Strutt,' she whispered.

'I know,' Mum whispered back. 'It's like a dream come true, isn't it?'

'My friends are going to die of envy when I tell them,' India went on.

'And my husband is already going green with jealousy,' laughed Mum. Dad rolled his eyes at the rest of us.

And that brought breakfast to an end. Zak disappeared upstairs. Finn and I went off to help India look after Fudge, so we were outside when we heard the scream, the crash, the thunderous

pounding, and the
yells that grew louder
and louder. Eventually
they burst out of the
house in the shape of
Manley Strutt clutching
a towel round his body,
hotly pursued by a whirly,
wet, orange monster.

'HEELLLPPPP!'

(That was Manley Strutt.)

**'HOOO HAAAH
HOOOOO HOOOEY
CHK-CHK-CHK-
CHK!'**

(That was Batpants,
waving a wooden
back scrubber from
the bathroom in
the air.)

You'd have thought Batpants was trying to murder the film star, but she was just playing. Everyone knew that except Manley, who thought he was under attack. Batpants made several attempts to grab Manley's towel, much to my parents' amusement. They were doubled up with laughter. Finn, of course, was jumping up and down and adding to all the yelling and screaming.

'I saw his b —' Mum slapped a hand over Finn's mouth in the nick of time, while India and I giggled ourselves silly.

Meanwhile Manley had whizzed up the stairs to the tree house and shut himself in. That was no good at all because Batpants knew every entrance in and out of that house. Within seconds she had climbed through a window. Manley gave a squeal of terror and came hurtling back down the steps.

'Do something!' he yelled as he went racing past us, closely followed by a galloping orang-utan going hoo hoo hoo. I was sure she was grinning.

'Give her your towel!' shouted Mum. 'It's the only way to stop her!'

'The towel?' shrieked Manley as he went charging past us for the third time. 'But that's all I've got!'

'If you don't give it to her she'll take it from you anyway,' Dad laughed.

'But, but, but,' went Manley, as Batpants closed in on him. He dived behind the tree and a moment later the towel came flying out in the ape's direction. Batpants stopped, bent down, picked it up, examined it all over, put it round her waist like a skirt and came wandering back to us, showing off her new item of clothing as if she was in a fashion parade. We fell about.

Dad found a pair of trousers and took them across to the tree. Manley's arm reached out gratefully and a minute later he sheepishly stepped into the open.

'It was unbelievable,' he told us. 'I ran the bath and went off to get ready. I came back and was just getting into the bathtub when I realized Batpants was sitting at the other end waving a scrubbing brush at me. She reached out to grab the towel and I guess I just flipped.'

'She likes a chase,' Mum said.

'And she liked your towel even more,' I added and everyone fell about again. Even Manley grinned. He could have got really cross but he was pretty good natured about the whole thing. He's just not used to so many animals. I suppose it is a bit odd to look out of your bedroom window and see an elephant in the garden – not to mention the donkey, the cats and, of course, Batpants.

Dad took Manley back into the house. 'You go and have your bath. We'll keep Batpants occupied out here. Then I suggest we all wander into town. There's a nice little coffee place where we can go and relax and you can forget all about your nightmare morning.'

'That's a great idea, Aslan,' said Manley. 'I'll be fifteen minutes or so.'

* * *

There are several cafés in town but our favourite is Luigi's. He's the owner and he's Italian and he does proper Italian coffee. I don't like coffee but I do like the smell of it and all the machinery they use to make it. The best thing about Luigi's is the cakes. Finn and I adore them.

Zak keeps trying to pretend that he's too grown-up for cakes now but what's the point in that? Adults aren't too old for cakes, so how come Zak is?

Luigi's has got tables on the pavement and we all sat outside. It wasn't long before we noticed that people were staring at us. Other people sitting nearby kept looking across at our table. Some of them edged their chairs closer, especially the women. And they were all looking at the same thing – Manley Strutt. He'd been recognized.

Eventually one of them came across and asked for his autograph. Of course, as soon as one person had done it, another came and another. Soon there was a queue. And a bit of pushing and shoving.

The rest of us found ourselves edged more and more to one side as Manley almost disappeared beneath the excited crowd of onlookers. The word quickly spread.

'Manley Strutt's at Luigi's drinking coffee!'

'Manley Strutt's in town!'

'Have you seen Manley Strutt? He's at Luigi's! It's true! I've just got his autograph – look!'

That's how it went. More and more people came over. There was a queue down the street and the biggest throng was forming round Manley himself. Soon there were so many people we lost sight of him. We could just hear his voice from time to time saying things like, 'Hey! Please don't all push at once. Can you give me a bit of space? I can hardly breathe? Hey!'

And then suddenly the crowd went wild. Dad and I were knocked off our chairs. Mum had to hide under the table to escape the pushing and shoving. We tried to get to our feet, but got pushed back down.

Eventually we managed to stagger upright and the big bustle had disappeared leaving just the long queue and – and – where was Manley? He was nowhere to be seen. We dashed inside Luigi's but he wasn't there. We raced back out and scoured the High Street, but Manley had definitely vanished.

Dad stood there, looking up and down and scratching his head in confusion. I could almost see the blood drain from his face as a terrible thought took hold of him.

'I think Manley's just been kidnapped from right under our noses,' he declared.

'Cool!' said Zak, and then realized it wasn't the best reaction. 'I mean crazy. That's crazy. Why kidnap Manley?'

'Money,' Dad said grimly. 'He's worth millions. They'll demand money – or else.'

Dad's mobile rang. It was as if time stood still. We stared at Dad. Nobody moved. The phone rang and rang until Dad slowly pulled it from his pocket and put it to his ear.

'Yes?'

He listened intently for what seemed like ages. At last he switched off and put the phone back in his pocket. Mum slipped an arm round him.

'What was that about?'

'It was strange,' Dad murmured. 'I don't quite

understand. A man was talking to me, but in a deliberately squeaky voice, like something out of a bad film. He said keep clear of the police. We are being watched –'

Our heads instantly swivelled in every direction, but it was ridiculous. We could have been watched from a thousand different places. Any one of the hundred or so people in the street around us could have been spying on us. Dad went on.

'He said if we go to the police then Manley will come to great harm. He repeated that several times and finally he said something weird. He said, "Go home. You will understand more when you get home".'

'What will we understand?' I asked. 'That doesn't make sense.'

'I guess we'd better get home and then maybe we'll find out,' suggested Mum. We began to walk, faster and faster. Soon we were running.

We raced towards our house. Had it been burgled? Had we been ransacked? Was the house on fire? Was another message waiting for us there?

As we reached home we couldn't see anything wrong. The front was fine. The door was still locked. There were no broken windows anywhere and no flames from the roof. All was as it should be. We dashed from one room to another, checking, but everything was fine and all was well.

'Noooooooooooooo!'

A scream came from the garden. It was India. She was in floods of tears. Dad dashed out to her.

'Fudge has gone!' India sobbed. 'They've taken my darling sweety-pops too.'

Blimey. Some kidnappers. They'd even managed to kidnap an elephant.

6.   Fantasti-bubbly-crumbo!

'How could anyone kidnap an elephant?' I asked.
'That's crazy!'

India was beside herself. 'Poor popsy! Anything
could have happened to her. She's on a special
diet, she needs the right food.'

Finn tried to raise her spirits. 'At least you won't
have to go round the garden picking up elephant
poo,' he pointed out cheerfully. It had quite the
opposite effect on India. She began flooding the
garden all over again, only this time with tears.

'My poor little twinkletoes!' she wailed.

I choked. *Little twinkletoes?* Fudge was an
elephant, not a dinky fairy.

Even Finn pulled a surprised face and then
stuck his fingers in his ears, which was hardly
surprising.

'There's Manley to think about too,' Dad said grimly, waving a piece of paper. 'I found this note in Manley's room.' Dad spread the letter on the table and we gathered round.

WE HAVE GOT MANLEY
AND THE ELEPHANT.
IF YOU WANT TO SEE
THEM ALIVE AGAIN
YOU HAVE TO PAY
£2,000,000.
WE WILL PHONE
INSTRUCTIONS.

And at that very moment the phone rang and we all jumped a mile. Dad put a finger to his lips but Batpants got to the phone first.

She held it up to one eye and squinted at it hard, as if she was trying to see who was at the other end of the phone. Dad danced circles round the ape trying to get it, but Batpants kept twisting and turning. She put it to her ear and looked at us with a rather superior kind of expression, like some fancy secretary in an office. Finally, she pursed her lips and spoke into the mouthpiece.

'Hooooo?'

I've no idea what the answer was but Batpants' eyes widened to the size of saucers. She yanked the phone as far from her ear as possible and

dropped it like a hot banana. Dad seized his opportunity.

'Hello? Yes. No. No. Yes. (Pause) We need time. We can't get £2,000,000 just like that. My piggy bank isn't big enough. (Pause) Of course I'm joking. This whole thing is crazy. You had better be looking after Manley and Fudge properly. (Pause) Yes, I know Fudge makes a lot of dung. She's an elephant. What do you expect? You have to clear it up yourself. (Pause). My daughter says you can make paper with it. And help save the world.'

Dad turned to me and whispered. 'They say they've got enough paper and they don't want to save the world.'

'Typical,' I muttered. 'That is so selfish.'

Dad went back to the phone, frowning. 'No, we won't go to the police. We'll bring the money. (Pause) Yes, tomorrow afternoon. You'll ring to let us know when and where. OK. (Pause) I want to speak to Manley. (Pause) He can't speak?

Why not? Because he's got a sock stuffed into his mouth. I see. Is it his sock? (Pause) Good. I'd hate to think he was sucking one of yours.'

Dad cocked his head on one side and looked at us. 'The line has gone dead. They've hung up.'

Mum clung to his arm. 'How are we going to find £2,000,000?' she asked. Dad shook his head and a determined look crossed his face.

'We're not giving them any money. We're going to find Fudge and Manley, and set them free.'

'Wow! Yeah! Fantasti-bubbly-crumbo!' yelled Finn, punching the air as he jumped up and down. 'We'll biff and baff them!'

'*Taisez-vous!*' I hissed at him. That's French for 'shut up!' Cool, eh? You should try it! (You say it like this: *tay-zay voo*.)

'Yes, calm down, Finn,' Dad snapped. 'We're not going to do anything hasty. Let's think this through. The kidnappers can't be far from here. They've had to move an elephant, so somebody must have seen or heard something!'

'We could ask around,' Zak suggested.

'Good idea.' Dad nodded. 'Let's see what we can find out. Take things step by step.'

'Poor popsicle,' murmured India, wiping her eyes.

'Don't forget Manley,' Dad reminded her. 'The poor guy is tied to a chair with a sock in his mouth.'

'Didn't they give him lunch?' asked Finn. 'That's horrible.'

'It's to make sure he can't shout for help,' Mum smiled, ruffling Finn's hair.

'Oh, of course,' he said, wishing he hadn't been so silly. 'We should tell the police.'

'That would be sensible, but we can't,' Dad explained. 'The kidnappers said that if we go to the police they'll harm both Manley and Fudge.'

'No!' squeaked India.

'I'm afraid so,' murmured Dad.

'Hooooooooooooooooooo!' moaned Batpants, leaping on to India's chest to hug her.

That would have been OK, but Batpants is heavy. India stumbled backwards, tripped on the sofa and went sprawling on to it with Batpants still clinging to her.

'Gerroff!' was the muffled squawk that came from beneath the shaggy orange pile.

'Snnnnnfffff,' snuffled Batpants, resting her head on India's shoulder and squeezing India's cheeks together until she looked like a punctured football.

'We're going to have to solve this ourselves,' said Dad. 'So let's see what we can find out. We'll start with the neighbours.'

We went out and began knocking on doors. Zak paired himself with India, of course.

'To make sure she's OK,' he said. 'She's upset.'

'No, she's not,' I said. 'She's been squashed and squeezed by an ape, that's all. You just want to have a big smooch.' And I made kissy-kissy noises at him. He stuck out his tongue at me. That's *so* grown-up for a teenager, don't you think?

The first people Finn and I asked live right opposite — Mr and Mrs Choo. It was Mrs Choo who opened the door. She looked at us rather stonily. Actually, it was more like cement than stone and her eyes were fixed on my height-of-fashion twig display.

'Oh. You're the girl who keeps pushing notes about dolphins and light switches through my letterbox, aren't you?'

I didn't think we were getting off to a good

start so I tried to change the subject.

'Have you seen an elephant?' I asked brightly, nice smile and all.

'Why, have you lost one?' Mrs Choo laughed, as if it was a joke.

'Yes,' said Finn seriously. 'Her name is Fudge and she looks like, well, she looks like an elephant.'

Mrs Choo eyed me closely. 'Your hair is full of leaves and twigs.'

'Yes. It's to show that I am environmentally friendly.'

Mr Choo came to join his wife at the door.

'They've lost their elephant,' Mrs Choo told her husband. She pointed at me. 'And she's environmentally friendly. You can tell by the twigs.'

'The elephant's called Fudge,' Finn repeated. 'She's got big ears, but not as big as an African elephant. Indian elephants have smaller ears, but African elephants have ears as big as – as big as –'

Finn's voice drained away. His eyes were fixed on Mr Choo's ears. Mr Choo's ears are MASSIVE. They're like satellite dishes stuck on the side of his head. He could probably pick up Martian TV with those ears.

'I didn't see an elephant,' Mr Choo told us. 'But I did see a lorry. It rattled the windows. I don't like those big lorries.'

'Oh. Well, sorry to have bothered you,' I said.

'You can stop bothering us with things about whales and wind farms,' Mrs Choo hinted. Her husband put a gentle hand on his wife's arm.

'It's their world too, you know. She's right to be concerned.'

I smiled at Mr Choo and decided that actually his ears were very nice, in a large sort of way. Nevertheless, I was disappointed. We turned to go and were halfway down the path when I had a thought. My brain was whirring. A lorry? Making the windows rattle? I hurried back just as the door was closing.

'Mr Choo,' I called. 'Was the lorry big enough to put an elephant inside?'

'Big enough for three elephants I should think,' he smiled.

'Hmmm. Can you tell me anything else about

the lorry that you noticed?' I felt like a detective, asking all these questions. Mr Choo thought so too.

'Yes, officer,' he said with a teasing smile. 'It was yellow and I think it was a removals lorry, the kind you use for moving house. It stopped just up the road there, not far from your house and it had the name of the company on the side: Packeederm Removals.'

'Thank you, Mr Choo.' I turned and ran after Finn.

'We're on the trail!' I told him. 'And it's red hot!'

'How do you know?'

'We've got to tell the others. Come on!'

Mum and Dad were going door to door with Batpants. The orang-utan had already scared three dogs and five cats. Mum saw us coming and sighed.

'Nobody seems to have noticed anything, but strangely enough they all seem to know you, Tilly.'

'Really?' I tried to look innocent. I'm pretty good at looking innocent. I guess it's because I've had to practise a lot.

'Yes,' Mum continued. 'Our neighbours seem to know an awful lot about dolphins, collapsing icebergs, saving electricity, saving whales, melting glaciers and so on. They tell me that most of their knowledge comes whizzing through their letterboxes when they're not looking – sometimes three or four times a day.'

'There's an awful lot to do to Save The World Mum. We can't just stand about and watch it all go wrong.'

'I know, darling. You're quite right. I was just a bit surprised – and I'm proud of you.'

I LOVE my mum! She is amazing.

But I had big news for them, and I quickly passed it on. By this time Zak and India had come to join us. They hadn't found out anything useful either, so I told everyone what Mr Choo had said.

Zak looked mighty suspicious. (Naturally – he's

suspicious of ANYTHING I say.) 'So, Mr Choo saw a lorry. How many lorries do you think come down our road? Hundreds, I bet.'

'I know, but this one stopped near our house.' My family looked at me and waited.

'It was yellow,' I added. They carried on looking at me, so I let them have it.

'There was writing on the side. It said PACKEEDERM REMOVALS.'

Zak snorted. Mum and Dad smiled. India raised her eyebrows and gave a happy little jump. Zak looked at them. He could tell something was going on.

'What?' he demanded. 'What?'

'Packeederm Removals,' I repeated. Zak was still in the dark. (He is SO uneducated. I mean, what kind of school does he go to?) India slipped one arm through Zak's and pulled him closer. Urrrghh! It must be like hugging a jellyfish.

'There's another name for elephants,' she told him. 'It's spelled P-A-C-H-Y-D-E-R-M, but you say it like this – *packeederm*.'

Finn grinned from ear to ear. 'Fantasti-bubbly-crumbo!' he breathed.

7. Batpants on the Trail

So, all we had to do now was track down the yellow lorry. That was not going to be easy. That lorry could have gone anywhere – north, east, south or west.

'The kidnappers would have to unload Fudge somewhere,' Dad mused, running a hand through his long hair. 'And it would have to be somewhere they couldn't be seen.'

'Mr Choo said the lorry went up that way,' I pointed.

'You can't unload an elephant into a house,' said Zak. 'And you wouldn't put it out in the open in case anyone saw it.'

'You're so clever!' India gazed at Zak with starry eyes. Oh dear. Surely she wasn't going to fall for my darling big sweety-pops brother? Zak grinned and tossed his long hair back from his head. (He loves doing that. He thinks it's cool, but actually it's so that HE CAN SEE WHERE HE'S GOING.)

'It would have to be a big shed, maybe a warehouse,' Zak suggested.

Bang! Mum slammed a hand on the table. 'The trade parks have warehouses. There are three or four of those round here.'

'Fantasti –' began Finn, but I got my hand over his mouth before he could finish.

'I'm fed up with you saying that all the time. Can't you think of anything else?'

Finn looked up at me, his face full of confusion. 'No,' was his simple answer.

At that moment Batpants came into the room with a lampshade on her head.

'Haaaaa, krrrrrrrrrrr,' she chattered, as she went swanning off round the table, like some top-notch model on the catwalk.

'You look splendid, Batpants,' said Mum.

'Here, have one of my handbags. Now go away and leave us in peace. We are busy trying to find Fudge.'

The ape left us, breezily twirling Mum's bag on her left arm and spinning the lampshade hat with the other. Peace descended once more.

Dad spread a local map on the table.

'This is what I suggest,' he said. 'Zak and India, you go and search the Oakhill Trade Park here.' Dad jabbed a finger at the map. 'Emma, you take Finn and search the Kildare Industrial Estate over here. Tilly and I and Batpants will try Riverside Trade Park.'

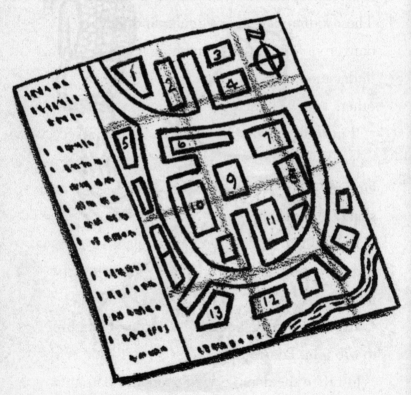

We gazed round the table at each other. My heart was already beginning to thump. It was pretty exciting. Suppose we actually *found* the elephant and Manley? What then?

Mum took control. 'Zak, you've got your mobile? Good. I've got mine and Aslan has his. We keep in touch, but listen carefully. These kidnappers are criminals and they're dangerous. We don't do anything if we see them, understood? If we find the lorry we ring the others and we'll meet up and decide what to do.'

'I'm cool,' nodded Zak, and I almost choked.

'No, you're not cool at all, Zak. You're more kind of like an ice cream that's melting fast – all sloppy and dribbling on to the floor.'

India stifled a giggle, while Zak glared at me so furiously I think he was trying to make me burst into flames.

'You're an ice cream, silly!' chortled Finn, just to rub it in. Poor Zak!

Just then the door banged open and Batpants

reappeared, this time wearing a wellington boot on the end of each arm. She had also tried to put a rubber glove on one foot. It flapped madly from her toes, like some strange duck trying to take flight.

Please don't ask me why she was waving wellingtons and rubber gloves at us. Batpants does things like that, OK? She's an orang-utan.

You try to explain why an orang-utan wants to do things like that. See? It's not easy, is it? Maybe she gets bored and has to find something to do.

I helped Finn remove the boots and glove. 'Dad, do we *have* to take Batpants with us? She is such a pain sometimes.'

Dad shrugged. 'We can't leave her behind.'

So that was that. We set off for different trade parks. Finn wanted to take his Ultra-Death-Mega-Zonic-Ray-Gun with him – the one that made a noise like six police cars having an argument, but Mum said definitely no way.

'But Mum, it's total death,' Finn told her.

'And it's totally not coming with us,' she warned. 'It's too noisy and will give us away.'

Finn heaved a long sigh. 'You'll regret this,' he observed wisely, as we split up and went in different directions.

We soon lost sight of the others and it was just me, Dad and Batpants against the Baddies. My heart was thumping again, even though I felt pretty safe with Dad. He's tall and strong, and I knew he wouldn't let us get into any danger.

Riverside Trade Park is pretty big with loads of different warehouses. There are two units that do building supplies. There's a big motoring place that sells windscreen wipers and batteries and oil and all that kind of yucky car stuff. There's a massive carpet showroom. Boring! Have you ever been in a carpet showroom? They are so DULL! In any case, we don't have much carpet at home

because of all the animals that go in and out of the house – know what I mean? Sometimes there are accidents of a wet nature, or even worse, a squidgy nature. Carpets and squidge do not go together well.

So, loads of warehouses and buildings and cars and vans and little roads that go down here and up there and round that, and so on. Lots of people too, wandering about pushing trolleys loaded with plants, or bits of wood, or carrying

long rolls of carpet. It was quite difficult to keep track of where we'd been. And all the time we were hunting for this big yellow lorry with PACKEEDERM REMOVALS written on the side.

Batpants was pretty well behaved, at least to start with. She held my hand and we went wandering about. Several people stopped to talk with us, although really they just wanted to stare at Batpants and speak to her.

'Is that your chimp?' asked one lady. I wanted to say, 'No, it's my pet frog!'

'What does he eat? Are they cannibals?'

'He's a she,' I grunted. 'She's not a cannibal. Maybe you mean a carnivore?'

The lady burst out laughing. 'Silly me! Of course. Carnival. Is she a carnival?'

I looked at Dad. 'Help!' I whispered in a little squeak.

Dad smiled at the lady. 'She's an orang-utan. They eat fruit and vegetables mostly.'

'Oh,' said the lady. 'One of them. There's one like that lives next door to me.'

'Really?' Dad was very surprised. 'Your neighbour has an orang-utan?'

The lady screamed with delight. 'No! He's a vegetarian. A vegetarian!'

Now Dad looked at me. 'Help!' he whispered back and we hurriedly moved on. A bit later Dad said, 'Some people can seem rather stupid, Tilly.'

'I know!' I cried. 'That woman was such a twit!'

'And when you meet someone like that you should always try to help them understand. If that woman knew more about orang-utans and understood them then maybe the world would be a better place and orang-utans wouldn't be in so much danger.'

I was silent for a long time after that. I was thinking. Dad was right. I decided that next time I met someone who seemed stupid I would be a lot kinder and try to help them understand.

Unless, of course, it was Zak. Or Finn. Or that lady again.

We had just about finished our search of Riverside Trade Park and hadn't found anything at all. We set off back home.

There was a thunderous noise coming from the tyre store as we walked past. Several cars were parked outside and men were working on two of them. They were using high powercd tools, taking tyres off the cars, putting them on machines and pumping air into them. Sometimes there would be a very loud *pop*! as a tyre suddenly jumped into the right shape. Batpants was fascinated.

Too fascinated. She suddenly broke away from me and went lurching up the slope towards the tyre store. The men dropped their tools double quick and went and hid in their office, peering out of the window as Batpants wandered round. I guess they thought King Kong had come to town. An orange, midget King Kong.

Dad and I hurried after her and tried to get
her but Batpants has an Olympic medal for NOT
BEING CAUGHT.

'Hoo hooo hooooo ha ha ha ha ha!'

You'd think she was laughing, listening to the
noise she was making. (I think she *was* laughing!)

She went zooming up the stacks of tyres. They
were piled high on one side of the warehouse,
dozens of them. Batpants wandered up and
down, bouncing on the tyres and generally
having a fine old time.

Some of the men who worked there began to come out. Obviously they were feeling a bit braver. They shouted at her to come down, calling her a monkey and all sorts. Dad tried to point out that she was an orang-utan but the men paid no attention. In any case Batpants doesn't like being shouted at. It upsets her, and then she starts to DO THINGS, and today DOING THINGS meant throwing tyres at people.

Batpants turned out to be a champion tyre-chucker!

She stood right at the top of the stack, frantically
hurling tyres down at us. Away they went, rolling

all over the place, knocking over people and
equipment, hurtling into cars and bouncing
down the street pursued by a yelling crowd.
You've never seen such mayhem!

In the meantime, Dad quietly sneaked up on her from behind and grabbed her by the hand. Batpants stopped, took one look at Dad and clapped her other hand over her eyes as if to say: 'Uh-oh! I'm in trouble now!' She's a scream!

Dad brought her down and we were busily telling the tyre people how sorry we were and it wouldn't happen again and all that rubbish, when Dad's phone rang. It was Zak.

'We've found the lorry!' he whispered into Dad's ear. 'It's here! Come quickly, and tell Mum!'

8. Disaster Strikes

Oakhill Trade Park was very different from the one Dad and I had been to. It was smaller, older and a lot more untidy. Riverside had flashy new buildings and lots of trees and grassy surrounds. Oakhill had rubbishy old buildings and not a single oak tree or hill in sight. In fact it had no trees at all. It was grimy, dull and a wee bit scary. It reminded me of warehouses I had seen in films. You know what I mean? You see big, dark buildings with shut doors and you know that something awful is hiding inside somewhere. That's what Oakhill felt like.

Mum and Finn were already there. Finn's eyes bulged with excitement.

'We've found the lorry!' he declared.

'Actually, *we* found the lorry,' Zak put in quickly. 'India and me.'

'Zak saw the lorry first,' added India. 'It made my blood run cold, but I felt a lot better when Zak gave me a hug.' India slipped her hand into Zak's. 'He's such a poppet.'

'A poppet?!' I creased up. 'He's more like an octopus if you ask me.'

India laughed. 'Your sister's funny!'

'Yeah,' muttered Zak. 'Funny peculiar – and believe me, Tilly is VERY peculiar. How many people do you know who go around wearing birds' nests in their hair as a fashion feature?'

'And how many people do you know who look like a zombie going to a zombie-party?' I answered.

'It's called being cool,' Zak snapped back.

'It's called being stupid,' I sniped.

'OK, you two, that's enough,' said Dad. 'We're not here to start World War Three. We've got a film star and an elephant to rescue. Where's the lorry, Zak?'

My brother (the zombie one) pointed to the largest warehouse, a crumbling wreck of a building in the far corner of the trade park. It was mostly made of corrugated iron, with a few dirt-smudged windows and big, sliding doors.

'The lorry is behind there. It's empty. We saw the back open and took a peek inside.'

Dad nodded. Batpants tried to climb up him and suck his ear but Dad wasn't in the mood. He'd gone very serious which meant he was thinking hard.

Zak screwed up his nose, which meant he was thinking too. He does that sometimes – I mean *think*. He does have a brain somewhere. It's just that it doesn't get used a lot, probably because so much of it is taken up with thinking about GIRLS.

'Packeederm Removals,' he murmured. 'It's a funny name for a removal company. It's almost as if the kidnappers wanted us to find them.'

Dad turned sharply. 'Really? You think so? Why would they want us to find them?'

Zak shrugged. 'I don't know. It just feels odd.'

Dad nodded and told us he was going to take a look at the building more closely and then report back to us. We watched him zig-zag across to the warehouse, keeping by the fence so he was less likely to be seen.

India gazed at Zak with sparkling eyes. 'Zak's always thinking of something,' she said, with stomach-churning admiration.

'I bet he is,' I muttered, and Mum nudged me hard with her elbow.

'You wait till you're his age,' she smiled. I took a step back and fixed my mum with my stoniest stare.

'I can tell you now, Mother, that when I am Zak's age I will NOT be looking for a SNOG

110

with a BOY, or anyone else for that matter, thank
you very much.'

Did that have the effect on Mum that I
wanted? No. It only made her burst out laughing.
Parents. Huh. Will they EVER understand?
Probably not.

We waited in silence until Dad came back.

'There's a door at the back which is loose. I think I can force it open. I'll go in first and if it's safe you can follow.'

'What about Batpants?' Mum asked. We looked at the orang-utan. She returned our gaze and calmly picked her nose.

'I'm not sure she's going to be much help,' Mum sighed.

'We can't leave her outside,' I said.

'We can't take her inside,' Zak argued. 'She could give us away. One hoot from her and we're done for. We don't know what might be inside.'

Batpants looked at Zak and put a big hairy hand across her mouth, just as if she was saying: 'I'll keep my big mouth shut'.

India solved the problem. 'I'll take her in with me and if she gives us any trouble I'll bring her out again.'

Zak was worried. 'I don't want you getting into danger,' he said, putting a comforting hand on her shoulder. He's so sweet, isn't he? NOT!

'Zak? Excuse me – there are several other people here,' I pointed out. 'What about your poor little sister and even smaller little brother? Aren't you worried about them?'

'No.'

Was I gobsmacked? Not in the least. That's Zak for you. Huh.

'Look,' Zak went on. 'If anyone sees you, Tilly, they'll die of fright on the spot. And they won't bother with Finn because he's just a small kid.'

'No I'm not!' cried Finn. 'I'm almost eight.'

'Finn, you won't be eight for another eleven months – that's almost a whole year,' said Zak.

Finn was about to protest but Dad held up his hand.

'Any more arguments from you three and we shall have to go straight home. Are we going to rescue Manley and Fudge, or not?'

'Rescue!' Finn and I chorused.

'I don't mind rescuing Fudge,' muttered Zak.

Obviously he wasn't too worried about gorgeous hunk, Manley Strutt. Dad ignored him.

'Good, no more talking then.'

'Yeah, *taisez-vous*,' I added.

Dad eyeballed a warning at me. 'Follow me,' he growled.

Bit by bit we made our way towards the warehouse, edged behind it, and there was the big yellow removals lorry. I studied the name on the side. Packeederm Removals. Maybe Zak was right. It was an odd name for a removals

company. Rats. I hate it when Zak's right.

The door that Dad had found was small and battered and made of metal. It looked as if an army had taken turns at trying to kick it down. It squeaked horribly as Dad pushed his weight against it and then it grated open. Batpants gave a low moan, but India quickly put her hand over the ape's mouth and she stopped. We listened for any sounds from inside but all was quiet.

'Wait here,' Dad whispered. 'I'll come back for you if it's safe.' He vanished inside.

We stood out there by the door for what seemed like ages, our ears straining for the least little sound. Our eyes kept flicking round the deserted trade park in case someone came, or a car arrived. We were keeping watch and worrying about Dad. He was taking such a long time. I had the strangest feeling that it was like being in a film; that it wasn't real at all.

But it was. It was only too real. A storm of noise burst from inside the warehouse. Shouts and running steps. Things crashing over, yells and thuds, bangs. Somebody cried out. Then slowly the noise lessened and all went quiet again.

We looked at each other. Now we were facing a disaster of mega proportions. We had lost our leader. I glanced at the others. We must have looked like a bunch of ghosts – everyone had turned white. My heart was almost falling out of my mouth. The silence crushed us, pressing in like a huge weight. Even Batpants look scared. She was hiding behind India and trying to make herself look small and invisible, which is pretty difficult if you're a large, orange, hairy ape.

'Mum, what do we do?' I croaked. 'The kidnappers must have got Dad. He's not coming back, is he?'

Mum threw her arms round Finn and me. 'No, darling. He's not coming back. It's up to us now.'

'We'll have to go in after him,' Zak announced grimly, flicking back his hair for added effect. Mum nodded.

'I'll lead the way,' she said. 'If we run into trouble the best thing we can do is to split up. We should all run in different directions. The kidnappers will never be able to chase all of us, so at least one of us will escape. Whoever escapes, go to the police.'

'Why don't we ring the police now?' asked Finn, clinging on to Mum's left leg.

'It's too dangerous. The kidnappers said if we call the police they will harm Manley, or Fudge, or your father, or even all of them. We don't go to the police until we absolutely have to. If we can get them freed without the police it will be much better. Keep quiet, keep out of sight, and if we get rumbled, run for it.'

'I knew you should have let me bring my Mega-Zonic-Ray-Gun,' Finn complained.

Mum gave him a brief smile then pushed her

way through the door, quickly followed by Zak,
India and Batpants. I grabbed Finn's hand and
held it tightly.

'Ow,' he squirmed.

'*Taisez-vous!*' I hissed back and pulled him in
after me, heart pounding.

9. All About Thursday

It took several seconds to get used to the dark. Batpants flung one arm round my left leg and clung to me. She was also hanging on to India with her other arm, so basically it was almost impossible to walk. We shuffled along with the orang-utan between us, making little moany noises.

'Mmmm-ooooo-eeeem-eeem-eeeeeemmmm!'

The ape was slowing us down. We couldn't call after the others and soon they had disappeared up ahead. Once we lost sight of them we didn't know which way to turn. They could have gone anywhere. A shiver of fear grabbed my spine. Batpants clutched my leg even more tightly.

'Oooooooo-eeee-oooooo-eeee!'

'Shh,' I hissed at her. 'Will you please stop sounding as if you want to go to the toilet.'

Batpants didn't like being told off. She slowly turned her head towards me, puffed up her cheeks, pressed her lips together and went: *Pfffff!* That was her way of showing me she wanted to shoot tomatoes at me!

The warehouse was full of ancient bits of

equipment and giant packing cases piled up into higgledy-piggledy mountains. Shafts of light streamed down through a scattering of dusty roof windows. It all made for a pretty spooky place, full of dark corners where anything might hide, waiting to pounce.

And then we saw Dad, and Manley, and Fudge – AND THE KIDNAPPERS! They were all in a clearing in the centre of the warehouse.

Dad and Manley were tied to chairs. They had

socks stuffed into their mouths. And they looked really uncomfortable. Dad was struggling angrily as one of the gang tightened the ropes that bound him to the chair. Fudge had a rope looped around one leg, with the other end attached to a rusty iron pillar supporting some kind of platform above. Keeping watch over them were four thugs, big burly men, with bulging muscles, and balaclavas pulled over their faces.

I can tell you my stomach was doing

somersaults. This was bad – really, deeply BAD.
I whispered to India. 'What do we do now?'

She shook her head. So did Batpants. She moaned again and looked at me accusingly as if to say: 'Why have you brought me to this horrible, dark, dangerous place?'

'We'd better try to find the others,' I suggested.

India nodded and we stared around, trying to decide which way would be best. Should we go to the left or the right?

'Left,' said India, just as I whispered, 'Right'. So that was a good start.

'OK, make it left,' I agreed, just as India said, 'Right is fine with me.'

In the end it was Batpants who made the decision for us. She suddenly opened her mouth and howled with despair.

Have you ever heard an orang-utan howl? When they are in their native jungle in Borneo you can hear their howls from miles away. The noise travels that far. Miles! IT IS VERY LOUD!

And now Batpants opened her mouth to the heavens.

'HOOOOOOOO-WAAAAAA-HOOOOOO-WAAAAAAAAA!!!'

The guards spun round and stared straight at us. One of them reached into his jacket and pulled out a gun. A GUN! I saw Dad try to get to his feet, but of course he couldn't.

'Run for it!' I yelled. India went crashing off one way, while I did the same but in the opposite direction, banging into boxes, tripping over things, heart hammering and feeling more scared than a mouse stuck in a snake pit. Behind me I could hear Batpants howling and crashing away too.

I pushed my way into a narrow space between two piles of crates and hid. I felt SO alone, as if the whole world was after me. I took deep breaths to calm myself down. Noises came from every direction. The gang had spread out and were shouting instructions to each other.

'You go that way!'

'I am! Take a look in that corner. I saw something move.'

'Why don't we all shut up and listen? They're bound to give themselves away.'

'Just find them!' someone yelled really angrily, right next to me. I jumped a mile. It was probably the boss-man, and he was just the other side of the packing cases that were hiding me.

Suddenly there was a lot of scuffling and a triumphant cry from the other side of the warehouse.

'I've got one!'

I peered round the corner just in time to see a fat man dragging India out into the open.

'Let me go, you filthy moron!' she screamed. Wow! That made a change from 'poppet' and 'sweety-pie'! She was trying to kick at his legs and even got in one or two, but he threw her on to her back, grabbed her by an ankle and dragged her across to Dad and Manley.

Fudge was getting pretty upset and tugging at
her rope. She didn't like to see her best pal India
treated badly. But the elephant was tied to the
iron pole and all she could do was make it shake
a bit.

That was when I spotted Mum.

SHE WAS WALKING ALONG A ROOF BEAM, MILES ABOVE THE GROUND!

I've no idea how she got up there. She must have climbed up somewhere and now it looked like she was a mile high, balancing on a tiny metal beam, half running, half walking. No wonder she's the world's best stuntwoman. She made it look so easy. If I'd been up there I would have frozen with fear. I'm not very good with heights.

I held my breath. Suppose she fell? Suppose she was spotted? My heart was in my mouth.

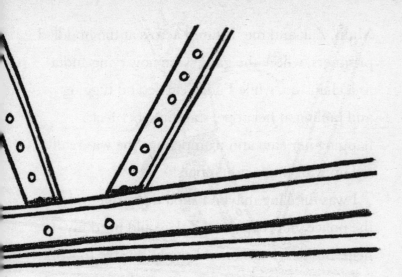

No – actually I think it had fallen right out of my
mouth. One kidnapper had a gun. Maybe the
others had them too. If the gang saw where she
was, it would be curtains for her. I was so scared
and proud – what a ridiculous feeling! My mum
is the bravest person in the whole world and I
wanted to be up there too, no matter how scared
I was.

I had to think. Who was left? It was up to
Mum, me, Zak, Finn and Batpants. Well, the last
two wouldn't be any use, so really it was down to

Mum, Zak and me. I stared across at the huddled prisoners, where the gang were now tying India to a chair too, while Fudge carried on tugging and pulling at her rope, stamping her feet, flapping her ears and trumpeting. She was really fed up with those kidnappers!

I was thinking maybe I should slip out and get the police, but Mum and Zak would need my help. Besides, I reckoned I might be able to work my way round behind the gang and their row of prisoners. If I could get to Fudge maybe I could set her free. That would cause havoc, for sure!

I took a deep breath and edged out of my hiding place. I was so tense I thought I'd snap in half, but I managed to creep round behind a big generator – well I think it was a generator, it was big and metal, that's all I remember. Zak could probably tell you what it was because he's a boy. They know useless stuff like that.

Finally, I found myself behind the prisoners. I ducked down. If I wanted to get to them I would have to crawl across four metres of open space with no cover. The same if I tried to reach Fudge. It was a huge risk.

On the other hand – well, there wasn't an other hand. I didn't have any choice.

I looked up. Mum was still working her way across the roof beams, but now she had a companion – Batpants! The ape was up there with her, calmly swinging along as if it was the sort of thing she did every day. I suppose it was, in a way. The roof beams were her jungle branches.

Mum was way too busy concentrating, so she had no idea where I was and I had no idea what she was planning. As for Zak and Finn, there was no sign of them. Maybe they'd scooted for home.

And then, just as I was thinking exactly that, Finn came strolling out into the open with a big grin on his face.

'It's a boy!' snapped one of the guards.

'Hi!' Finn answered, still smiling. 'What are you doing?'

'What do you mean, what are we doing?' repeated the guard, puzzled. 'What does it look like we're doing? In any case, what are *you* doing?'

'I want to show you my earwig,' said Finn. 'He's called Thursday, cos that's when I found him. My sister said I should call him Thursday Afternoon, but she's stupid. And did you know, he's got really big pincers? He looks as if he'd like to gobble up big beasties but actually he only eats plants like daisies and stuff.'

And Finn just stood there talking to them, just

like that! Talk about brave! I was so proud of him, even if he did tell them I was stupid. And he just went on and on. 'And did you know, they use their pincers for fighting each other. And did you know, they're nocturnal which means they come out at night. And did you know –'

I suddenly realized that this was my chance. The gang were all watching Finn, completely captured by his lecture on earwigs. I crept forward as quickly as possible. *Creep creep creep*, slithering across the floor like a snake. Actually, it was a pretty filthy floor and it wasn't very nice sliding along like that. I was getting very grubby.

Meantime, Finn kept the kidnappers chatting but they were closing round him, getting suspicious.

AND THEN A HAND SUDDENLY GRABBED MY ANKLE! I froze absolutely solid with terror, top to toe. Finally, I managed to peep behind me.

Zak! It was big bro! He must have been hiding

pretty close to me, waiting for Finn to distract the gang. Now he was creeping up too. He pushed his long hair out of his eyes, flashed a grin at me, and together we wriggled our way behind the row of chairs. I started to work on Dad's bonds while Zak had a go at India's.

We had to duck down behind the chairs a couple of times when the gang glanced our way, but luckily nobody saw anything. At last we got the ropes loose. Dad rose to his feet, muscles tensed and ready for action. His chair scraped the ground. The guards swung round.

'Don't budge!' shouted one, marching towards us. India screamed and threw herself at Zak, burying her head in his shoulder. She would!

Now, all four of the gang had surrounded us. Talk about feeling like a burst balloon. My plan – Zak's plan too – had failed miserably. We had both been captured. Great.

'SKRREEEEKKKKKK- SKRANNNGGGGG- SKRUNNNKKKK!'

The terrifying noise made us all whirl round to look behind us. Fudge was going mad with fury. She was tugging at her rope so hard that the rusty pole she was attached to was now bending and giving way. The platform above her was threatening to come crashing down. Fudge's ears flapped angrily and she filled the warehouse with her trumpeting.

'BLARRRRRR-BLARRR- BLARRRRRRRR!!'

'Don't move!' screamed one of the gang. 'And someone stop that blasted elephant!'

'You leave sweety-pie alone, you monsters!' India shouted.

'Shut up, girlie!' snarled boss-man.

'I've lost my earwig,' Finn blurted. 'Has anyone seen Thursday?'

'Just shut up, you stupid kid, or you won't see Thursday, Friday, Saturday or any other day of the week!' yelled the boss.

And then –

SHREEEEEKKKKK-KER-SPLANGGGGG!!!

The platform above Fudge finally gave way as the furious elephant pulled out the support column. The platform collapsed and the crates stacked up on it came tumbling down, smashing to the floor and breaking into a thousand pieces.

The guards leapt out of the way, but they still had their guns and they were training them on the elephant on the loose, and there was no way to stop them.

10. Surprised? You're Telling Me!

SHWOOOOOOOOSSSSHHHH!

Mum seemed to come from nowhere, swinging

through the air on the end of a rope,

like Tarzan but without the loin

cloth and all that stuff. She

came arcing down, feet first

and –

BEDDUNNKK!
CLUNNGGG!!!
OOOFFFFF!!!!!

The gang went down
like ninepins as she
smashed into them. Only
one was left on his feet and
already he was swinging his
gun round on Mum, taking aim
as the rope carried her across to
the other side of the warehouse.
And then –

SPLODDOINNGG!

This time it was Batpants doing the
Tarzan act. The orang-utan came swinging
down at a high speed. As she swooshed
overhead she let go and dropped *slap bang*
down on the last guard's head. The gun went off
harmlessly and they both fell to the floor and had
a gigantic wrestling match.

Never wrestle with an orang-utan! They
are incredibly strong. Besides, they'll probably
suffocate you with their long hair, if nothing else.
Batpants was soon sitting on top of a whimpering

guard. And as if that wasn't enough action for
the day –

SPLINNGGGG!

Bright spotlights suddenly flooded the whole
warehouse and more voices began shouting.

'Cut! That was brilliant! Utterly, utterly brilliant!
The best bit of action film we've ever done!'

Out of the shadows a figure emerged – a short, fat man with a thick beard, thick black spectacles and a big grin. He shook hands with Dad AND THEN HE SHOOK HANDS WITH ALL THE KIDNAPPERS! WHAT WAS GOING ON?

Dad flung an arm round me and hugged me close. 'You were great, Tilly. It was all perfect.'

I pushed him away, completely confused.

'I don't understand, Dad. What's happening?'

Manley was going round and grinning at everyone. 'Boy, that was quite something. Kids, you were fantastic.'

Mum joined us. Both my parents were smiling broadly. 'Sorry,' began Mum. 'We couldn't tell you because it wouldn't have worked out. We had to keep it a secret.'

'KEEP WHAT A SECRET?' I shouted. 'I DON'T UNDERSTAND. WILL *SOMEONE* PLEASE TELL ME WHAT'S GOING ON?'

'We've been making a film,' said Mum. 'Dad told you he and Manley and India were working on a film with Fudge. Well, this IS the film. The kidnappers are actually actors working for the film company.'

Dad looked at me while I let all this sink in. So it had all been a trick. It wasn't real. They were making a film. Huh! So all the time I'd been scaring myself to death it was for nothing. Just play-acting.

'Thanks a million, everyone. I thought you were all in deep danger. I really thought that. I was frightened and worried and thought you might die. I even thought *I* might die. I was even worried about Zak, for heaven's sake! Now it turns out it was all a sham.'

Dad hugged me again. 'I know, honey. Sorry, but it was the only way we could be sure we would get a good performance from all of you.'

I frowned. 'What performance?' I asked.

'You and Zak creeping up to untie us. All that stuff with the guards and so on. We weren't sure how you would actually do it, but we knew you would do something, and of course Mum and Batpants were in on it too.'

'So even the orang-utan knew! But not us kids!' I blurted angrily.

Mum tried to stroke my hair to calm me

down but I wasn't having any of that and pulled away sharply. 'We wanted you children to be in the film,' Mum explained. 'And we wanted you to think it was real so you would believe in what you were doing. You children are going to be starring in the film.'

I might have known Zak would be impressed. He is won over so easily and now he was walking on air.

'Wow – I'm in a movie. I'm going to be a star.'

'You're already my star, swccty-pic,' gushed India. 'You saved me from that horrible gang and cut me free.' India tilted up her head and kissed him. Could things get any worse? Yes, because Batpants saw the smooching couple and decided that she wanted to kiss ME! Urrrrgghh!

Well, that's what happened. That's how Finn and Zak and I came to star in a film. (Not to mention Thursday the earwig, who had hidden in Finn's pocket when it all got too noisy.) We even went to the premiere and walked on the

red carpet and gave autographs and everything.
So did Fudge and Batpants. They were the
biggest stars of all and everyone loved them.

After the film we were all taken out for a meal
at a really flash restaurant. I mean, they even
had linen napkins! Manley Strutt was there and
all the big stars of the film, plus Mum and Dad
and the kidnappers that weren't kidnappers,
and India. Sadly we couldn't fit Fudge in

and she had to stay behind, but Batpants was allowed to join us.

'She's very well behaved,' Mum told the waiters, keeping her fingers crossed.

Batpants sat between India and Manley and showed everyone how good her table manners were. She even wiped her mouth with a napkin! Mind you, she also wiped India's mouth, and Manley's, and anyone else's mouth that she could reach with her long hairy arms.

Then she discovered the olives. There were several bowls of olives on the table for people to pick at. Do you like olives? I don't. They look like rabbit droppings and taste like them too as far as I'm concerned. Mum says it's a grown up taste and I'll like

148

them when I'm older. Huh. I don't think so.

Anyhow, Batpants took a bowl of olives and
tipped the whole lot into her mouth. She chewed
a little and a strange expression came over her
face. Finn and I have seen that expression before.
We looked at each other and grinned. Sure
enough Batpants' cheeks began to swell up. They
bulged more and more and more until suddenly –

RATTA-TATTA-SPLATTA!!!

A stream of black olives came shooting from
her mouth like bullets, spraying the entire table
and the other side of the restaurant. People
screamed and fell backwards off their chairs.

Manley Strutt clawed at the table and managed to bring that down with him. The entire dinner splodged everywhere, especially on top of Manley. Half the guests were screaming and yelling about their ruined clothes, their ruined hair and their ruined handbags. And every time Manley Strutt tried to struggle to his feet he skidded on the food-covered floor and fell back down again.

It was the biggest mess I have ever seen in the whole of my life and it was BRILLIANT! Batpants loved it too. She jumped up and down, waving her long arms in the air and shouting to the sky in triumph.

'Hoo hoo hoo HAAAAAAAAH'!

I don't think Batpants will be asked to make another film for a while! (But I hope we are.)

It all started with a Scarecrow.

Puffin is seventy years old.
Sounds ancient, doesn't it? But Puffin has never been
so lively. We're always on the lookout for the next big
idea, which is how it began all those years ago.

Penguin Books was a big idea from the mind of
a man called Allen Lane, who in 1935 invented
the quality paperback and changed the world.
**And from great Penguins, great Puffins grew,
changing the face of children's books forever.**

The first four Puffin Picture Books were hatched in 1940 and the
first Puffin story book featured a man with broomstick arms called
Worzel Gummidge. In 1967 Kaye Webb, Puffin Editor, started the
Puffin Club, promising to **'make children into readers'**.
She kept that promise and over 200,000 children became
devoted Puffineers through their quarterly instalments of
Puffin Post, which is now back for a new generation.

Many years from now, we hope you'll look back and
remember Puffin with a smile. **No matter what your age
or what you're into, there's a Puffin for everyone.**
The possibilities are endless, but one thing is for sure:
whether it's a picture book or a paperback, a sticker book
or a hardback, **if it's got that little Puffin
on it – it's bound to be good.**